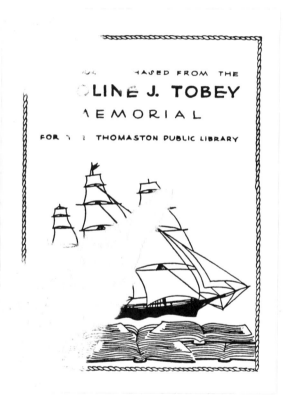

Punished!

by David Lubar

DARBY
CREEK
PUBLISHING

Text copyright © 2006 by David Lubar
Cover illustration by Chris Sheban
Illustration copyright © 2006 by Darby Creek Publishing

Cataloging-in-Publication

Lubar, David.
Punished! / by David Lubar.
          p. ; cm.
ISBN-13: 978-1-58196-042-5
ISBN-10: 1-58196-042-5
Summary: Logan and his friend Benedict are playing tag in the library. Logan gets
caught when he runs into a mysterious man. When Logan doesn't apologize sincerely,
the mysterious gentleman punishes him by causing him to speak in puns. Only finding
seven examples each of oxymorons, anagrams, and palindromes within the time limits
will return Logan to normal.
1. Boys—Juvenile fiction. 2. Friendship—Juvenile fiction. 3. Word games—Juvenile fiction.
[1. Boys—Fiction. 2. Friendship—Fiction. 3. Word games—Fiction.] I. Title. II. Author.
PZ7.L96775 Pu 2006
[Fic] dc22
OCLC: 61050749

Published by Darby Creek Publishing
7858 Industrial Parkway
Plain City, OH 43064
www.darbycreekpublishing.com

Printed in the United States of America

1 2 3 4 5 6 7 8 9 10

For Uncle Ben,
who passed along to me
his passion for puns;
and for Joelle,
who graciously endures
the results.

Contents

CHAPTER ONE

Bound for the Library

✳

"This is a terrible idea," I told Benedict as we walked up the stone steps toward the huge wooden door. "We could be having fun." It was wonderfully warm outside—a perfect day for tossing a baseball around.

"It's a great idea," Benedict said. He dashed ahead of me and yanked the door open.

"But we have two weeks. The reports aren't due until the end of the month." I left the beautiful May weather behind and followed Benedict into the cool darkness of the old building. The half-dozen lamps scattered around the floor tried their best to brighten the place, but the tall ceiling soaked up most of the light.

"It's way too soon to get started," I said as the door closed behind me.

"We've got half days next week," Benedict said. "If we do our reports now, we'll be free then. Trust me, Logan. This is a good idea."

"I get it," I said. "You're trying to be picked as Student of the Month." As long as I'd known him, Benedict had wanted that—especially since the award came with a coupon good for a free super-deluxe pizza from Zio's Kitchen. I'd won the award last January, but I promised myself I'd save my coupon for the perfect summer day. That would be the day I hit my first home run of the Little League season. Perfect pizza, perfect hit, perfect day—it would be worth the wait.

I didn't think Benedict would ever have to figure out when to use a pizza coupon. One way or another, no matter how hard he tried, he always messed up before the end of the month.

"I've got a real shot this month," he said. "I can almost taste that pizza. Especially since I'm going to write such a great report—as soon as I figure out a good subject."

"Come on. Let's just get this over with." There was no way I'd admit it to Benedict, but his idea sort of made sense. Our teacher, Mr. Vernack, had assigned us reports. We had to write five whole pages on the topic: "What's So Great about Being a Human?" As far as I was concerned, I could answer that in one word. Baseball. But I had to fill five pages. And we couldn't just make stuff up. Mr. Vernack said we were supposed to use at least three different sources, not counting the Internet. That meant stuff like books and magazines—which, naturally, meant the library. So Benedict and I had come here right after school.

We walked past the towering rows of bookcases in the adult area and through the hall that led to the kids' department. I didn't expect we'd stay very long. Benedict has a hard time sitting still. So do I, but he makes *me* look calm. Even so,

I thought we'd stay for more than five minutes.

I was wrong.

When we got to the kids' area, I grabbed a couple of baseball books from the shelves in the sports section. I knew right where they were because I always checked to see if they'd gotten any new ones in. I love 796.357. That was their Dewey decimal number. I opened the first book and started to flip through it when, *WHACK*, Benedict ran past, smacked me on the back, and yelled, "Tag! You're it."

He dashed down the hall. I had no choice. It's impossible to sit still once you're tagged. Totally impossible. It's like if someone sings, "Row, row, row your—" and then stops, you just have to finish it by singing, "boat." I chased him. He didn't head back to the adult section.

Instead, he made a sharp left and raced down the stairs to the basement.

I followed. A sign near the steps said: REFERENCE SECTION. By the time I reached the bottom, Benedict had vanished among the shelves. But I could hear his footsteps. I rushed after him. "I'll get you!" I shouted.

I reached the end of the aisle. From the echo of his footsteps, it sounded like he'd turned right. I swung that way and caught a glimpse of him as I hurried to the end of the next aisle.

"Slowpoke!" he called.

"Oh yeah?" I put my head down and pumped my legs hard, running full force. Benedict might be fast, but I knew I could catch him.

I didn't even see the old guy until I crashed into him.

CHAPTER TWO

Running into Trouble

"**O**oofff," I said as I bounced back from the collision. A quick glance at the man showed me I hadn't done any damage. He barely even looked surprised. "Sorry," I said as I started to run around him.

He put out a hand and stopped me. "This is a library," he said, staring at me through the bottom part of those glasses that have a line right across the middle of each lens. "Not a playground."

"No kidding." I hate it when people tell me obvious stuff. I wondered if he worked in the library. I'd never seen him before, but I didn't pay much attention to the people outside the kids' area. He was an old guy, dressed kind of like a teacher, with a jacket but no tie. He had a book in his other hand—the hand that wasn't keeping me from chasing Benedict.

"Hey, I said I was sorry," I told him.

"Words aren't always enough." He glanced at the books that surrounded us and let out a small chuckle. "They should be, but they aren't. That's a lesson you obviously haven't learned yet. Maybe you need to be punished."

Punished? My stomach squeezed tight as

his words sunk in. Was he threatening me? I backed away from him and got ready to make a sprint for the stairs.

He didn't try to stop me. Instead, he nodded and said, "Yes. Punished. I suspect it would do you some good." He raised the book he was holding and blew on it. A puff of dust swirled through the air. I closed my eyes as the dust tickled my face.

"Hey, cut it out!" I wiped my face with my sleeve and then opened my eyes. He was gone.

WHACK!

"Tag again!" Benedict shouted, running up from behind and giving me another slap on the back.

"Cut it out," I said. I glared at him so he'd know I wasn't fooling around. "You almost got me in trouble." I rubbed my eyes. They still felt dusty. I blinked hard. Everything looked funny for a moment, like I was seeing through someone else's eyes. But after another hard blink, things looked normal again.

"Sorry," Benedict said, but he couldn't keep from grinning. He started to climb one of the bookcases.

"Will you please try to behave your shelf?" I said.

"What?" he asked.

"Behave yourself," I told him again.

We returned to the kids' section, and I got back to work. Benedict worked a tiny bit, too, but mostly he ran around until Mrs. Tanaka, the kids' librarian, told him to stop. Then he sat for a while. Actually, he sat for thirty-eight seconds.

I know, because I counted. Then he ran around some more. He reminded me of one of those old wind-up toys that are all shaky and jerky. The kind that will stop so it looks like they've run down, then jerk back to life and start moving again. But Mrs. Tanaka took it easy on him. She's pretty nice. She never shushes us. And she's always seeing if she can help us.

While I was working, she came over and asked, "Did you find everything you needed?"

"Yup," I told her, "Eyebrows the books all the time to see what's new."

She smiled. "I browse the books all the time, too. I really enjoy it."

"Alphabet that you do," I said.

She laughed like I'd made a joke. "I'll bet I do, too."

"I don't see what's so punny."

She groaned, then muttered, "Very punny." Shaking her head, she walked away from me.

I had no idea why she was laughing. Or why she was groaning. I took a few more notes, then got my stuff together and grabbed Benedict as he ran past my table, making airplane sounds.

"Ready to go?" he asked.

"Yeah. House about we head home?"

"Stop that," he said.

"Stop what?" I didn't understand what he was talking about.

But instead of answering, Benedict turned away from me and walked toward the door. I had no idea what was bothering him, so I just followed him outside.

When we got to the bottom of the steps, he said, "Want to come over and throw around the football?"

"Sure," I said. Benedict likes football as much as I like baseball, so we usually take turns playing each game. "We can tackle the reports later."

"Will you please knock it off, Logan? You're starting to sound like my Uncle Horace. And he's really annoying."

"Knock what off?" I wished he'd tell me what he meant. "If you expect me to hike all the way over to your yard, you'd better start making sense. Besides, I don't really field like football. Baseball is a batter game."

"Oh, just forget it," Benedict said. "Call me when you decide to be normal again." He walked off, slapping parking meters as he passed them and shouting, "Hi-i-i-i-yah!"

I had no idea why he was angry with me. I also had no idea that things were about to get a lot worse.

CHAPTER THREE

Bad Words

"**H**ow was the library?" Mom asked when I got back home.

"Okay." I took a deep breath through my nose. Mmmmmm. Something smelled great.

"I'm making pot roast," Mom told me.

I lifted the lid and peeked into the pot. "It smells totally stew-pendous."

"Can you stick this in the fridge for me?"

Mom asked, pointing to the dessert she'd just made. "It's your favorite flavor—butterscotch."

I took the bowl from the counter. It was still warm. "Sure. I don't mind pudding it away."

Mom stared at me for a moment. "We'll be eating in fifteen minutes," she finally said.

"The spooner you lettuce eat, the better," I told her.

I left the kitchen and headed to my room to drop off my backpack. Behind me, I heard Mom muttering something about me going through a phase.

I ran into Dad as I was coming out of my room. "Hey, Logan," he said, "don't forget we have some yard work to finish this weekend."

"Is there a lot mower to do?" I asked.

"Yeah," Dad said, giving me a funny look,

"there's a lot more to do. We need to put that fence around the tomatoes."

"Right. Weed need to be garden them from the rabbits."

Dad groaned and shook his head.

"What's wrong?" I asked. I was getting tired of all the groaning. Benedict had groaned at me. So had Mrs. Tanaka. Mom had groaned, and now Dad was groaning, too.

"Nothing," Dad said. "I guess I was just as silly when I was your age." He reached out and ruffled my hair the way he does when he talks about the good old days. Then he headed downstairs. I followed him into the kitchen.

My little sister Kaylee was already there. I sat, and we started to eat. But every time I said something, they all groaned and rolled their eyes up at the ceiling. Except Kaylee. She kept giggling.

I bent under the table and looked at Buster, my dog, who was waiting for me to slip him a treat.

Buster panted. That was a relief. "At leash my own dog doesn't groan at me," I whispered as I patted him.

Buster groaned.

Maybe it was really a yawn, but it sure sounded like a groan. I dropped a piece of pot roast on the floor for him anyhow.

After dinner, when we'd finished clearing the table, Kaylee came over to me, grinned, and said, "You're funny, Logan. Just like my cartoons."

"Thanks," I said, although I wasn't sure it

was a compliment. But she was the only one who wasn't groaning at me, so I figured I'd better take whatever nice words I could get.

And it turned out the problem followed me to school. I had trouble right away the next day. First thing after morning announcements, we had language arts, which is a fancy way to say English. There was a woman standing up front with Mr. Vernack. She was short and thin with a friendly face and long, black hair. "Class," Mr. Vernack said, "this is Ms. Glott. Say hello."

"Hello, Ms. Glott," we all said.

"She'll be joining our class for the next month as a student teacher," Mr. Vernack told us.

"I'm thrilled to be here," Ms. Glott said, giving us a big smile that made her look even friendlier.

"You'll find we have some very clever students," Mr. Vernack said. "And I don't think there will be any problems while you are here." He glanced at Benedict as he said that. "Now, let's get to work."

He pointed to the vocabulary list on the board. "Logan, the first word is *isolate*. Can you use it in a sentence?"

"Sure," I said. "I'm sorry isolate getting here."

Everyone started laughing. Everyone except Mr. Vernack. He frowned and gave me the next word. *Justice.*

"Justice I was leaving home, my dog got loose."

Mr. Vernack's frown grew so big, his eyes became slits. He said one word: "Decide."

"My dog chased a cat around decide of my house."

"Logan, is this some kind of joke?" Mr. Vernack asked.

"No, Mister Vernack. I was jest doing wit you asked." I clamped my mouth shut. Nothing seemed to be coming out right.

He stared at me for a long time. Then he sighed and said, "Very well, I'll give you one more chance. The next word is *industry*."

That was easy. There was no way I could mess it up. "The cat got stuck up industry and wouldn't come down."

I listened, as surprised as everyone else when the words came out of my mouth. I sure hadn't meant to say that.

Mr. Vernack spoke just two words of his

own. He pointed toward the door. "Principal" was the first word. "Now" was the second.

I walked down the long hall.

"What seems to be the problem?" Principal Chumpski asked when I stepped into her office.

I started to explain. But every time I said something, she chuckled. Then she started laughing. Finally, I sat back and waited for her to stop laughing.

"You're quite some boy," she said between laughs.

I nodded, afraid to open my mouth.

"Don't lose that sense of humor, no matter how much other people groan," she said after she'd managed to catch her breath. "But keep it to yourself in class. Mr. Vernack is a wonderful teacher, but I suspect he's never going to appreciate your talent for word play. Now go buzz on back to your room and behave."

"Thanks. I'll try to beehive myself." I got up from the chair and breathed a big sigh of relief.

Principal Chumpski started laughing again. Finally, she shook her head and waved toward the door.

As I left the principal's office, I thought about the strange stuff that had been happening to me. I hadn't noticed right away, but once I started paying attention, I realized one thing for sure: Words weren't coming out of my mouth the right way. They left my brain just fine, but after that they went horribly wrong.

I was so used to saying what I meant, I

had to listen carefully to catch the mistake. But there was no doubt. Every time I opened my mouth and said more than two or three words, a joke came out. No, not a joke. Worse than a joke—a pun. And people seemed to hate puns. They might laugh, but after they laughed, they groaned.

Why was this happening to me? It was almost like I was being punished.

Pun-ished!

Oh my word.

As I thought about the man in the library, a shiver ran down my spine. And then it ran back up. And then it slipped into my stomach and gave it a hard kick with a pointy boot.

Maybe you need to be punished.

Those were his words. He'd done this to

me. I had to go back to the library. That's what I'd do. As soon as school was out, I'd go find him. He had to be there. If not, I was doomed.

CHAPTER FOUR

A Confusing Explanation

I found him in the reference section down-stairs, sitting at a table and reading a book.

"Hey," I said as I walked over to him. "What did you do to me?"

"Shhhhh," he said. Then he glanced up and smiled at me. "Oh, it's you. Hello. I don't believe we've been properly introduced. I'm

Professor Robert Wordsworth." He held out his hand.

"Logan Quester," I said automatically as I shook hands with him.

"Wonderfully appropriate," he said.

That didn't make any sense, but I wasn't going to worry about it at the moment. I had more important things to learn. "What did you do to me?" I asked again. "Every time I open my mouth, a pun comes out." Except then, I realized. Maybe it didn't happen around him because he was the one who had punished me. If he had to listen to all my bad puns, I guess he'd be punishing himself, too.

"And you think that's my fault?" he asked.

"You said I should be *punished.*"

He nodded. "Perhaps I'm partly to

blame—but you have to admit you brought this on yourself. You weren't punished for no reason."

"Well, make it go away," I said.

"Sorry, I can't."

"Why not?"

"Only you can remove the punishment." He paused and tapped his finger on his chin as he stared up at the ceiling. "If I remember correctly, it takes three steps. It just so happens I might be able to help you with your quest." He reached in his jacket pocket and pulled out a small camera.

"What's this for?" I asked.

"Step one—bring me seven oxymorons." He handed me the camera.

"Oxy-what?" I asked as I took the camera.

It was heavier than it looked.

He reached in another pocket and pulled out a pen and a notepad. He wrote one word, tore off a sheet, and handed it to me.

Oxymoron.

"I have no idea what that means," I told him. "How am I supposed to bring you something if I don't know what it is?"

He ignored me and started reading his book again.

I pointed the camera at him and pushed the button. Nothing happened. Then I pointed it at myself. Still nothing. "It's broke," I said.

He glanced up from his book and shook his head. "You mean *broken*. If you have no money, you're *broke*. If the camera didn't work, it would be *broken*. It isn't. It works perfectly," he told me, "but only when you're taking the pictures you're supposed to take. Now, you'd better get going if you want to make any progress. You need to get all seven pictures within twenty-four hours." He pointed at the clock on the wall. The time was five minutes after four.

"Why?" I asked.

He shrugged. "Why doesn't *foot* rhyme with *boot*? Why are there two ways to spell *one* and three ways to spell *two*, but only one way to spell *three*? I didn't make the rules. But if you take more than a day, you can forget about ending the punishment." He turned away and went back to reading his book.

This was crazy. I had no idea what *oxymoron* meant, and it was obvious he wasn't going to tell me. I sighed and looked around at the shelves that surrounded us. "Of course," I said, hitting myself on the side of the head with my palm. "I can look it up."

I ran off to find a dictionary.

"No running," he called after me.

I grabbed a dictionary and looked up the word, even though I had a feeling it wouldn't be there. It sure didn't look like a real word. But it was. *Oxymoron.* It meant "a phrase containing contradictory terms." Great—I still didn't have a clue. On top of that, now I needed to look up another word to make sure it meant what I thought it did. I kept my place with one finger and thumbed through the dictionary to find *contradictory*. In my mind, I imagined going from one word to the next, until I had all ten fingers holding places like they'd been caught in some sort of awful paper trap, never finding out what anything meant.

But it wasn't that bad.

It turned out that an oxymoron was pretty simple—just a phrase where the two parts seemed to have opposite meanings. The dictionary gave some examples: "pretty ugly," "strangely normal," and "sweet sorrow." I got it. *Pretty* was the opposite of *ugly.* So, even though *pretty* meant something different when you said "pretty ugly," it still made you think of opposites. Even *oxymoron* was an oxymoron. It came from a couple of Greek words that mean "sharp" and "dull."

I had to admit the idea itself was kind of fun. It would all be really cool—if my entire future weren't in danger.

I tried to think of where I could get a picture of something made up of opposites. And not just one—I needed seven! Right off, I got an idea. I left the library and went down the road to the supermarket. It sold fish—all kinds of fish. It even had a tank with lobsters. And, if I was lucky, it might have something else.

Most places that sell fish sell shrimp, too. And *shrimp* also means "small." I went through the door and followed my nose to the seafood section.

They should call it the "smellfish" section, I thought. Sure enough, there in the case, on ice, were these really huge shrimp. And I saw the sign I'd remembered from last week when I went to the market with Mom and Dad: "JUMBO SHRIMP." *Shrimp* means "small" and *jumbo* means "big." That absolutely had to be an oxy-moron.

I pointed the camera at the shrimp, held my breath, and pressed the button. If nothing happened, I'd be in big trouble.

CLICK!

Big sigh.

One down, six to go.

CHAPTER FIVE

Opposites Attract

As I walked away from the fish department, I wondered if I'd find any other oxymorons in the supermarket. Dozens of foods flashed through my mind. "Cold hot dogs!" I said as the idea hit me. I ran to the cooler where they had all the packaged meats and tried to take a picture of a pack of franks.

No click. The camera didn't work. I started

to get worried, but then I realized the problem. "Cold" was the opposite of "hot," but it wasn't the opposite of "hot dogs." So while "cold hot dogs" might be a strange phrase, it wasn't an oxymoron.

As I wandered down the next aisle, I tried to think of words I'd find in the supermarket. "Fresh" was one. They used that a lot. "Fresh sour cream," I said out loud. But that wasn't any better than "cold hot dogs."

When I reached the ice cream, I watched a guy open the door, stare inside for a moment, then close it. That gave me a great idea. The inside of the door was frosty. I went over and wrote on it with my finger. *True lies*. That was an oxymoron. Feeling proud of my cleverness, I raised the camera.

No click.

I guess that was cheating. I had to find the oxymorons out in the world, not make them myself.

Then, as I scanned the rest of the aisles, I saw a display of paper plates, and—stacked up right next to it—glasses. Made of plastic. "Plastic glasses," I said, testing the feel of the oxymoron as I spoke it out loud. It felt right.

As I raised the camera, I was pretty sure it would work.

CLICK!

Thank goodness. That made two.

I found the third oxymoron without even looking for it. I was walking past the area where the store sold cooked food. It was like a small cafeteria right next to the deli section. I spotted two big soup pots. One held clam chowder, which I don't like at all. The other had chili. The sign above it read: "Red-hot chili." It almost didn't sink in at first. Then I got to thinking: *Chili* sounds just like *chilly*, which means "cold."

CLICK!

It looked like an oxymoron could contain a pun! The important thing was that I already had almost half of what I needed. I figured the rest would be easy.

After cruising all the aisles several times without finding anything else, I decided to hunt around town for the other four. I could always come back to the market later.

On the way out, I ran into Benedict.

"Hey, what are you doing with that?" he

asked, pointing to the camera.

"When someone lens you a camera, you have to snap up the offer," I said.

"Logan, this is getting ridiculous," said Benedict.

"Sorry. Wait," I said. "I'll give you a click explanation."

Maybe Benedict could help me. I told him what an oxymoron was and told him I needed to find four more of them for a project I was working on. I didn't say anything about the professor or about being punished. I didn't think he'd believe that part. The whole time I talked, the puns kept coming, but Benedict seemed to understand what I needed.

"I know," he said. "Don't try to think up the whole thing at once. First, you need to just think of words that describe stuff," he said.

"Yeah. Adjectives," I told him, remembering what I'd learned in language arts. I had to admit Benedict's idea was a good one. If I started with the right first word, it might make it easier to come up with a whole oxymoron. Benedict was pretty smart sometimes, even if he did think football was better than baseball.

Benedict nodded. "I know some. *Large, small, tiny, sharp, light.*"

"Hey, *light*. That's a bright idea," I said. I realized *light* meant two things. It meant "bright," but it also meant "not heavy." Maybe we could find an oxymoron using *light*.

"I know just where to look," Benedict said, snapping his fingers. He ran off. I followed him down the street to the lamp store.

"Good thinking," I said. "Watt a delightful idea."

Benedict groaned. "You'll have to go into the lamp shop by yourself," he said.

"Why?" I asked.

"The last time I was in there, they told me not to come back."

I pushed open the door.

"Be careful," Benedict said. "Most of the stuff they sell breaks real easily."

I walked inside, staying right in the middle of the aisles, as far as possible from the glass. I saw dozens of lamps with all sorts of different shades. I looked for dim lights or dull lights, but no oxymorons leaped out at me. I didn't even see anything that could be a heavy light.

I was about to give up when I realized I'd

been staring at an answer the whole time. "Light shade!" I shouted. Since a shade blocks light, I figured *light* was the opposite of *shade.* I raised the camera and pointed it at a wall of different kinds of lampshades.

CLICK! Four down. I wondered how many other oxymorons I'd missed.

"The lamp shop was a brilliant suggestion," I told Benedict when I got back outside.

He groaned, then said, "Hey, let's try the hardware store. They have tons of stuff."

"Great. Let's lumber over there and see if we can nail down a couple oxymorons," I said.

Benedict let out a groan that was loud enough to be a scream. He shuddered and shook his head, but he didn't run away.

We went down the block to the hardware

store and started looking around. One section was filled with all sorts of stuff for hanging things on walls. And there it was—a package labeled "straight hooks."

That will make five, I thought. I raised the camera.

CLICK!

Now I only needed two more. Benedict and I searched the rest of the hardware store, and then ran around town until dinnertime, but we didn't find anything else.

"Well, I'll see you in school," he said when we'd arrived at his house.

"Lesson I see you first." I waved and headed home.

That evening, I couldn't believe how many oxymorons I heard. They seemed to pop up everywhere. Of course, I'd never known about them before. But the ones I heard at home weren't the kind I could take pictures of.

"Careful," Mom told Dad when he was wrapping up some meat to put away. "If you don't seal it tightly, it'll get freezer burn."

Freezer burn, I thought. Unfortunately, everything in the freezer was wrapped up, so there wasn't any freezer burn to photograph.

There was an ad on the TV for a radio station that played soft rock.

Then Dad talked about a boxer he knew who was a light heavyweight.

Oxymorons were everywhere. But I still needed two more.

After dinner, I searched all around the house for oxymorons. I even opened our dictionary and tried to take a picture of the samples they had under the definition. No luck.

In the middle of all this searching, Kaylee came up to me with a book in her hand. "Read me a story?" she asked. She loved books. And she loved drawing pictures. So she especially loved picture books.

"Sure." I figured that would be safe. Besides, I was ready for a break. I sat on the couch with her, opened the book, and started reading.

"Puns upon a dime, deer were tree litter pegs." Oh boy, none of it was coming out right.

But Kaylee giggled and snuggled up next to me. "Don't stop. I like the way you read it."

So I read her the rest of the book and then returned to my oxymoron hunt. I searched until it was time for bed. But I didn't have any luck. When I went back to my room, I tried to find out how bad my punishment really was. From what I'd seen—or heard—so far, I knew I could say a really short sentence without making a pun. I closed the door and then said, "Hello."

No pun. Okay, so I could say one word. I tried two. "Thank you."

That worked. "I am Logan," I said.

So far, so good. "It dozen always happen," I said. Shoot. It looked like three was as high as I could go. I tried again, just to make sure that four was my limit. "One, two, three, floor." It looked like that was it. I got into bed and went back to thinking up oxymorons.

As I lay with my eyes closed and my head

on the pillow, I felt as if I were trying to fall asleep inside a dictionary. *I'm in big trouble,* I thought. But that was nothing new.

"New!" I said as I sat up in bed. That word gave me an idea. I rushed to the garage. We had a ton of newspapers stacked up against the back wall for recycling. You could call them "old news."

CLICK!

Just one more. But I was totally out of ideas.

As I went to sleep, I realized I wasn't just out of ideas. I was also in running out of time. If I didn't find my seventh oxymoron by the end of the school day, I'd be punished forever.

CHAPTER SIX

Slowly Running Out of Time

As I sat in school the next day, every tick of the clock seemed like an explosion. Time was racing away. I kept reaching into my pocket to make sure the camera was there.

"Still looking for oxymorons?" Benedict asked when we sat down in the cafeteria for lunch.

I nodded. As much as possible, I was trying

to keep my mouth shut. I held up my index finger to show him I just needed one more.

"How about *cafeteria food*?" he asked. "Anything they serve in this place really isn't food."

That was funny, but I didn't know if it was a real oxymoron. I checked around to make sure nobody was watching me, then took out the camera, aimed it at the slowly hardening mass of gunky macaroni on my plate, and pushed the button.

Nope. No luck.

"Is it broke?" Benedict asked. I guess he'd noticed it hadn't clicked.

"Broken," I said, automatically, just like Professor Robert Wordsworth had said to me. I shook my head. "Nope."

When we got back from lunch, Ms. Glott took over the lesson. "I love words," she said. "There are so many ways to have fun with them. I'll be sharing a lot of that with you while I'm here."

I stopped listening. I was desperately searching the room for that last oxymoron. I ran every adjective I could think of through my mind. *Tall, short, big, little, slow, fast,* and tons of others.

Nothing.

I could feel sweat trickling down my forehead. *Dry sweat?* No. *Fast trickle?* No. *Soft forehead?* No, no, no.

The bell rang. I checked the clock. Three-thirty. It would take me half an hour to get to the library. And I only had until 4:05 to find my last oxymoron.

As I walked toward the door, I glanced over my shoulder at the front desk. Mr. Vernack was talking with Ms. Glott. They were laughing and discussing onomatopoeia. Normally, I'd be happy to have such a fun student teacher, but I had too much on my mind right now. I needed that last oxymoron.

"*Student teacher*!" I shouted, smacking myself on the forehead. I couldn't believe I'd been searching all over the place when the answer was right in front of me. *Student* was the opposite of *teacher.* I whipped out the camera and pointed it at her.

Ms. Glott glanced over toward me and smiled.

Please, I thought as I pressed the button.

CLICK!

Whirrrrrrr.

It sounded like some gears were turning inside. I left the classroom and hurried to the library.

"Seven oxymorons," I said, putting the camera down on the table in front of the professor.

He took the camera and slipped it into his pocket. "Did anyone help you?" he asked.

I thought about Benedict running around with me. I guess he tried to help, but I'd been the one who'd found the oxymorons. "Sort of," I admitted.

"Do your own work from now on," he said. "If you tell anyone too much, you might never be cured."

He reached into another pocket and pulled out a small, cloth bag that was tied at the top with a piece of gold string.

"Seven anagrams," he said.

I took the bag from him. It felt just like the purple cloth they used for the curtains on the school stage, except it wasn't dusty. "What are anagrams?" I asked.

He gave me an annoyed frown. "And where are we? And what do we have all around us?"

"I know," I said. "Look it up."

I headed for the nearest dictionary, wondering how hard this task would be.

CHAPTER SEVEN

Scrambling for Answers

It sounded simple once I checked the definition in the dictionary. Take a word. Use all the same letters to make another word, and that's an anagram. Like *slow* and *owls*, or *teach* and *cheat*. Some words had a bunch of anagrams. *React, trace, crate,* and *cater* were all anagrams of each other. And it could be done with more than one word. *New York* could be anagrammed into *worn key*.

But how, I wondered as I walked out of the library, was I supposed to put an anagram in the bag? I stared at the bag, trying to figure out how it worked.

"What in the world are you doing?"

I looked up when I heard Benedict's voice and jammed the bag into my pocket.

"I just have an errand to ruin," I said. "I'll ketchup with you later. I mean, I'll sketch up with shoe later. No, I'll scratch pup with who. I mean—oh, fur jet about it." The more I talked, the worse it seemed to get.

Benedict groaned and shook his head. "You won't get rid of me just by making stinky jokes. If I can survive my Uncle Horace, I can handle anything. Besides, I know what's going on."

"You do?" I felt a flash of guilt, like when Mom caught me trying to hide the vase I broke.

Benedict nodded. "You're looking for words again, right?"

"Anagrams," I admitted, feeling relieved that he didn't know more than that. I explained what they were.

"What do you need them for?"

"Same project." I started to walk down the street.

"Look, I'm in school with you all day. I've never heard of any project like this." He stepped in front of me.

"Not for school." I said, stepping around him. It was rough trying to keep all my answers short.

"Want help?" he asked, stepping back in front of me. "I was going to work on my report, but this would be more fun."

"No, thanks," I said. It would have been great, but the professor had warned me not to get any more help.

"Some friend you are," Benedict said. He turned away and stomped up the library steps.

"Wait!" I called.

He just kept walking.

Great. Now he was mad at me. But there was nothing I could do about it right now. I had to find seven anagrams. I started thinking up all the short words I could and seeing if they had any anagrams. *Place?* No anagrams I could find. *Table?* There was *bleat*. That's what they call the sound a lamb or a kid makes. I knew that because my grampa had a farm with sheep and goats. But I didn't think there was any such thing as a *table bleat* or a *bleat table*. I kept thinking. *Scale laces, west stew, lemon melon, rat art.*

"Rat art!" I said. That could be a picture of a rat. I just hoped it didn't mean a picture that a rat drew. I'd never have a chance of finding something like that. But where could I find a picture of a rat?

Kaylee liked to draw. And she loved animals. I ran home, went up to her room, and asked her if she had any drawings of rats.

Kaylee nodded. "Yup. I love to draw them. They're so cute." After digging around for a minute, she pulled out a nice picture of a white rat eating a hunk of Swiss cheese.

"You art so talented. Can I burrow the rat?" I asked.

"Sure. You can have it." She handed me the picture and ran off.

I pulled the bag out of my pocket. As I started to put the picture near the opening at the top, I felt a tugging, like the bag was a giant magnet and the drawing was a paper clip. I let go of the drawing and—*SWOOSH*—it got sucked inside the bag.

One down. Six to go.

I had a great idea. I went downstairs and dug through the box of games in the living room. We had one game called Scrabble that used wooden tiles with letters on them. Mom and Dad played it all the time. I started pushing the tiles around, looking for anagrams.

Hey, *tile* and *lite* were anagrams. I picked up one of the tiles. It didn't weigh much. I tried to put it in the bag, but it wouldn't go.

"Duh," I said as I realized my mistake. I'd done the same thing last year on a spelling test. No matter what it might say on food boxes and menus, the word wasn't spelled *l-i-t-e*—it was *l-i-g-h-t*.

But I kept playing around with the letters and came up with a bunch of ideas. Whenever I got one, I wrote it down on a piece of paper. Speaking of which, *piece* didn't have any anagrams that I could find. Neither did *paper.* I figured I'd never find some of the things on my list, like a *rock cork*, since that didn't make much sense. Neither did *door odor, shoe hose,* or *glass slags.* I figured a *taco coat* would be hilarious, but I knew there wasn't any chance I'd find one. And if I tried to make one, I was sure I'd mess up the whole kitchen. But I wrote down every single anagram I thought of, just in case.

A couple of times I got so close to good ones, it drove me crazy. Like with *apple*. You can use most of the letters to spell *peal*. But then I realized I had two problems. I had a letter left over, and I'd spelled the wrong kind of *peel*.

After I had a long list, I ran around looking for things that would fit the ideas. My quest took me from the basement to the attic.

There was a box of old dishes in the basement. I remembered we used them when I was little, but Dad kept complaining that they were too ugly to eat off of. So Mom put them away. I hoped I remembered right. I searched around until I found the box. Yup—I was in luck. And yuck—I had to agree with Dad about them being ugly. The plates were decorated with roses. Lots of roses. *Petal plate,* I thought. Flowers were made of petals. I picked up a saucer and held it near the bag. *SWOOSH.* That made two. Five to go.

I ran through the rest of my list. The easiest one was *cat act.* When I first thought of it, I wasn't sure I could find anything. But Dad had taken me to the circus last year, and he bought me a souvenir program. There was a picture of the lion tamer. That was definitely a cat act. I tore the page out of the program and let it get sucked into the bag. *SWOOSH.*

In the fruit basket, I found a *cheap peach.* The price sticker was still on it. *SWOOSH.*

I figured that was it for the fruit bowl, but then my eyes fell on something else. Mom had bought some tangerines. And, according to the sticker, they were from Argentina. "Wow," I said out loud as the letters clicked together in my head. "An *Argentine tangerine.*" I had to admit I was really proud of that one.

That made five. Just two to go. I was on an anagram roll. And I knew exactly where I'd get the last two. I went to the freezer and pulled out the bag of French fries. Mom always bought the same brand: 'Tater Treats. Not quite an anagram if you use the whole bag. There was an extra *s.* But, take just one, and you had a *'tater treat.* Perfect. I pulled out one of the stiff, frozen pieces of potato and fed it to the bag. *SWOOSH.*

Then I went to my room. I had lots of old

plastic toy animals, including a couple of horses. I dug through the box in my closet, looking for the right one. There was this book about a horse that lived near the ocean: *Misty of Chincoteague.* I had a model of her. Since she lived by the seashore, that made her a *shore horse.*

"Hay, I'll sea ya, Misty," I said as I held her over the top of the bag. "I'm a bit saddle see you go, but Mom's been nagging me to get rid of my old stuff anyhow."

SWOOSH.

Made it. Seven anagrams.

This sure had been easier than the oxymorons. Or maybe I was just getting better at it.

At least I didn't spend the next day in school all distracted because my mind was dancing through the dictionary. But I still tried not to talk in class.

"What do you think, Logan?" Mr. Vernack asked me a couple of times during the day.

I just shrugged. I wasn't going to take a chance that the puns would get me in more trouble.

Benedict ignored me. I realized he was angry, but I hoped he'd get over it.

Ms. Glott, the student teacher, started to tell us how much she liked words. "Does anyone know what an oxymoron is?" she asked.

My hand shot up. I yanked it back as quickly as I could. No way was I opening my mouth.

She looked at me for a moment. "Did you raise your hand?" she asked.

I shook my head and tried to look con-fused.

"I know," Benedict said. He smirked at me and gave the definition—the same one I'd told him just the other day. He even mentioned the part about it being Greek. That was fine—if he needed to show off, I wasn't going to stop him.

"Impressive," Mr. Vernack said. "*Very* impressive." He almost never repeated himself. I could see he was suddenly thinking about Benedict as perfect student-of-the-month material. Maybe Benedict would finally win that pizza he wanted so badly.

Ms. Glott went on to tell the class about oxymorons and anagrams and a couple other things. The coolest one was redundancies. Those were words you didn't need. Like when people talked about a *free gift.* Since a gift is always free, you don't need the extra word. Another redundancy was *unexpected surprise.* A surprise is always unexpected. Also, *pre-recorded.* Anything that's been recorded has obviously been pre-recorded. She pointed out that *pre-* and *previous* were often redundant. I hoped my next task was redundancies, because now I'd have a head start. Or a pre-start.

Then Ms. Glott told us some of her favorite words, including *serendipity.* That was what you call it when you find something you aren't looking for—kind of like being at the right place at the right time. I thought about the Argentine tangerine. Talk about serendipity. Of course, right now, I couldn't talk about anything.

After class, I went across town to the library. *What if he's not there?* I wondered as I hurried downstairs to the reference section. Was there a word for when you don't find the thing you're desperately looking for? *Neresdipity? Dipitsereny?*

But he was right at the table.

"Seven anagrams," I said as I handed him the bag.

He bounced the bag up and down in his palm for a second, as if weighing it, then nodded and said, "Very good."

"What's next?" I asked. "Redundancies?"

"No. Nothing that easy." He reached into his shirt pocket, pulled out a handful of rubber bands, and dropped them on the table. They lay there looking like exhausted worms. "Seven palindromes," he said.

"What's—" I caught myself as I picked up the rubber bands. *That should be a snap.* I grinned, and then groaned as I realized I was even making puns in my mind now.

I headed for the dictionary and looked up *palindromes.* It turned out they were very cool. But the more I thought about them, the more I realized they might not be that easy.

CHAPTER EIGHT

Either Way, It's the Same

The definition was simple. A palindrome is a word or sentence that is spelled the same forward and backward. The names *Otto* and *Hannah* were each palindromes. I didn't know any Ottos or Hannahs. I guess a palindrome was actually a special kind of anagram. But this was the cool part—a whole sentence could be a palindrome, too. Like *Madam, I'm Adam.*

This might be tough.

"Think small," I told myself as I walked home. I started running small words through my mind. I'd already used *rat art* for an anagram. I wondered if there was anything called *rat tar.* Yuck—if there was, it sounded pretty disgusting.

When I got home, I flipped through my dictionary, looking for short words. That's how I came up with my first palindrome. As soon as it hit me, I jumped up and ran to the kitchen.

This isn't going to be hard at all, I thought, feeling pretty pleased with myself.

There were plenty of pots. And plenty of tops. *Pot top.* If you spelled it backwards, it was still *pot top.* I grabbed the smallest pot top and slipped one of the rubber bands over it. I wasn't sure what was going to happen. I hoped the top wouldn't disappear. Mom wouldn't like that. But I shouldn't have worried. Instead of making anything vanish, the rubber band started to glow. Then the glow faded. And when the glow was all gone, the rubber band had changed from brown to yellow. I slipped it off and put it in my pocket.

This was great. One down and just six to go. All that stood between me and a normal life was a half dozen more palindromes. I thought about slipping another rubber band over a different pot top, but I was so close to ending my punishment, I didn't want to take any chances doing something that might be cheating.

I realized I had two palindromes living at home with me. Mom and Dad. Mom was easy.

"Want to see a magic trick?" I asked.

"Sure." She was in the middle of balancing the checkbook.

"First it's brown." I slipped the rubber band over her wrist. "Now it's yellow."

"Very nice." She smiled at me and went back to what she was doing.

Dad would be tougher. If I showed him the trick, he'd want to know how it was done. Luckily, he always took a nap after dinner. As soon as he had drifted off on the couch, I sneaked over with a rubber band and put it on his finger. Yellow!

That made three. I thought about all sorts of short words. I started playing with the Scrabble tiles again. *Bed deb, tin nit, pen nep.* None of them worked. There wasn't anything like a *car rac* or a *rac car* either. But as I stared at the letters, I realized there was something even better. I went back to my closet, searched through the old toys, and pulled out a model racecar. I slipped a rubber band around it and smiled as the band changed color.

Four down, three to go. In less than half an hour, I found two more. Dad had a level in his toolbox. *Level* was a palindrome all by itself. And then I realized my sister Kaylee could be called *Sis* for short. And she loved magic tricks. So I did the rubber band trick for her.

That made six. But as easy as it had been to find the first six, I had no luck at all finding the seventh. I felt like a home-run king in a batting slump. I'd knocked a bunch of pitches out of the park, and then I couldn't hit another ball. I flipped through the dictionary. I played with the letter tiles. I closed my eyes and ran words through my head until my brain felt like it was turning into alphabet soup.

"I'm doomed," I told Buster when I went to bed.

"Woof," he answered.

"Woof foow," I said, checking it to see if it was a palindrome. Nope. "Bark krab." Nope again. "Roof foor." Nowhere near close enough.

The next morning, I felt like I hadn't gotten any sleep at all. *Sleep,* I thought. I turned it around. *Peels.* Was there such a thing as *sleep peels?* Nope. It was just another useless phrase to add to the endless list of things that didn't work.

I trudged off to school and took my seat.

"Still mad?" I asked Benedict when he sat down.

He didn't answer me.

"If you're not mad, we could anger round together this weekend."

Benedict turned his back toward me.

I decided to shut up before I drove him from the room. This was awful. If my best friend hated me, how would strangers treat me? I thought about what my life would be like if I didn't find the final palindrome. I'd never be able to talk to anyone again. People would just groan at me and stop listening. Everyone would hate me. They wouldn't take anything I said seriously. I'd have to live someplace where nobody spoke English. They wouldn't understand me, but at least they wouldn't hate me.

The day dragged on. As it got close to three-thirty, I decided all I could do was go to the library and give Professor Wordsworth what I had. Maybe he'd give me more time, or a different task. Either way, it was my only hope.

I glanced at the clock again. One minute to go.

"Well, Logan," Mr. Vernack said, walking over to my desk. "You've been extremely quiet these last few days. I'd like you to join the discussion. We don't want Ms. Glott to think you don't like our lessons." He pointed to the chalkboard. "Please pick one of those words and use it in a sentence."

I stared at the list on the board. *Device, conduct, example, satellite, protest.* It didn't matter which word I picked. Any one of them would doom me when it turned into a pun. Whatever I said, Mr. Vernack would get angry. My best chance was to keep my mouth shut.

"I want an answer from you right now," he said. "Or you can stay after class."

After class! Oh no! If he kept me after, I'd never get to the library on time. I had to say something. But Mr. Vernack was so angry now that I knew he'd make me stay if I said a pun.

I was doomed either way. I sat there with my mouth open.

"MY PANTS!" Benedict screamed. "My pants are on fire." He leaped from his desk and ran toward the front of the room. Then he started jumping up and down and slapping at his legs with both hands.

Everyone stared at him.

He kept slapping for a moment, then glanced down and said, "Wait. My mistake. Never mind."

As Benedict walked back toward his seat, he grinned at me. Right then, the bell rang. Everyone started to rush out.

"Okay, okay, class dismissed," Mr. Vernack said. "Except for . . ."

I held my breath.

"Benedict," he said.

I guess imaginary burning pants were a lot worse than not answering a teacher. I slipped away and ran out of the building. "Thanks, Benedict," I said to myself as I raced down the school steps and headed for the sidewalk. What a pal I had. I owed him a lot.

But I was still in trouble. I reached the library and went down to the reference section.

The professor was sitting there, reading.

"I have a problem," I said. I pulled the rubber bands from my pocket, one brown and the other six bright yellow, and held out my hand to show him.

"So I see," he said.

"Can I get more time?" I asked.

He shook his head. "No. Sorry."

"I've looked everywhere," I said. "It's not fair. It's just not fair."

He stared at me calmly, and then said, "You still have a few minutes. Maybe the answer is right under your nose."

"Lip?" I asked. "*Lip pil?*" I said, trying to make a palindrome out of it.

"That was just a figure of speech," he said. He leaned forward until his face was only inches from mine. "Maybe the answer is right in front of you." He reached out with one finger and touched the end of my nose.

I took a step away. Then I froze as the answer sank in. Of course.

"Professor Robert Wordsworth," I said, remembering the day he'd told me his name.

He smiled.

I stretched out the rubber band. "And I'll bet your friends call you . . . ," I said as I slipped the rubber band over his hand.

"*Bob!*" we said together.

What a simply wonderful palindrome.

The rubber band on his wrist glowed yellow.

Behind me, the clock ticked. I glanced at it. Five minutes after four.

"Am I cured?" I asked.

"Find out for yourself," he told me as the sound of running footsteps announced Benedict's arrival.

"I figured I'd find you here," he said, sliding to halt next to me. "The way you rushed out the other day when I saw you on the steps, I knew something important was going on. Even if you wouldn't tell me about it."

I took a deep breath and spoke. "Thanks for saving me back there in school. Did you get in much trouble?" Wow. Not a single pun. I wasn't being punished anymore!

"Nah," Benedict said. "Mr. Vernack just gave me a lecture about civic responsibility and made me clean the chalkboards. But I guess I can forget about being student-of-the-month for a while."

"Would you settle for being friend of the century?" I asked.

"I guess that's pretty good, even if it doesn't

come with a pizza."

I grinned at him. "Who said it doesn't? Let's get one right now. I have that coupon, remember?"

"I thought you were saving it for a special day," Benedict said.

"You have no idea how special today is. So how about we go stuff our faces?"

"Sounds great," Benedict said. "Now, are you going to tell me what all of this was about?"

"Sure," I said. I glanced at the professor. He nodded, so I figured it was okay. "It's a long story."

"Best told someplace else," the professor said. "This is a library, not a meeting room."

Benedict glanced over at the professor. "Who asked you?"

Oh no.

The professor raised his dusty old book

and took a deep breath.

Here we go again, I thought, expecting Benedict to get punished. I wondered if he'd get the same three quests or have to find something completely different.

Instead of blowing the dust, the professor winked at me, put the book down, and went back to reading.

"Come on," I said, tugging Benedict by the arm. "I'll tell you all about it on the way to the pizzeria."

We walked out of the library, back into the warm weather.

"I'll share mine with you when I win it," Benedict said.

"Thanks."

"I know I messed up for May. But June's a

short month. It'll be easy. Especially when I turn in a great paper."

"Did you figure out a topic?" I asked.

Benedict nodded. "I've got something Mr. Vernack will love. Ms. Glott, too. I'm going to write about words and stuff."

"Oxymorons and anagrams?"

"Those are okay. But I really want to write about puns. I know they make people groan, but there's also something sort of cool about them."

"Yeah. They are kind of cool," I said. "Ready for pizza?"

"Sure, *Pete's-a* great guy," Benedict said.

"Yeah, *Pete's-a* great guy." I groaned. And then I laughed. And then I said, "Since we have a coupon, we don't *knead* any *dough*." I didn't have to make the pun, but that doesn't mean I didn't want to. It was nice having the choice.

"I never *sausage* a nice pizza," Benedict said when we reached the window outside the pizzeria.

"I read about one in the *news-pepper*," I said as I opened the door.

And we walked inside—two groan boys.

About the Author

DAVID LUBAR is a writer and video-game designer. He's written a variety of books for teens and young readers. His novel *Hidden Talents* was named an ALA Best Book for Young Adults. *Dunk*, a wildly funny young adult novel set on the boardwalk of the Jersey Shore, won the 2004 Young Adult Book Award from the Keystone State Reading Association and appeared on the Texas Lone Star Reading List. His other books include *Dog Days, Wizards of the Game, Flip, Sleeping Freshmen Never Lie, In the Land of the Lawn Weenies*, and his latest short-story collection, *Invasion of the Road Weenies*. His short stories have appeared in *Boys' Life, READ* magazine, *Nickelodeon* magazine, and in various anthologies, including *Sports Shorts* (Darby Creek Publishing).

David has designed and programmed many video games, including *Home Alone* and *Frogger 2* for the Nintendo GameBoy, *Fantastic Voyage* for the Atari 2600, and *Swamp Thing* for the Nintendo Entertainment System. His most recent game work has been for Nabisco's Candystand and Nabisco World Web sites.

A popular speaker who has appeared at national conferences and schools all across the country, David Lubar is a native of New Jersey, but he now lives just over the border in Nazareth, Pennsylvania, with his wife, daughter, and a trio of felines. He also lives online at www.davidlubar.com.